Rod Clement spent his childhood in New Guinea and on the north coast of New South Wales. After three years of study at Mitchell College in Bathurst, he managed to fail just enough subjects to get an Associate Diploma in Media Studies.

This award-winning author and illustrator of children's books also works as a full-time cartoonist for a major Australian newspaper. He has been published in Australia, America and Europe.

He has written and illustrated *Counting on Frank*, *Just Another Ordinary Day*, *Grandad's Teeth*, *Frank in Time*, *Olga the Brolga* and has illustrated *Edward the Emu* and *Edwina the Emu* (both written by Sheena Knowles).

Rod lives in Sydney with his wife and three children.

Angus&Robertson

An imprint of HarperCollins*Publishers*, Australia

First published in Australia in 2005
under the title *Louisa May Pickett, the Most Boring Person in Class*
Reissued in 2008 under the title *Louisa May Pickett's Best Show and Tell Ever*
by HarperCollins*Publishers* Australia Pty Limited
ABN 36 009 913 517
www.harpercollins.com.au

HarperCollins*Publishers*

25 Ryde Road, Pymble, Sydney, NSW 2073, Australia
31 View Road, Glenfield, Auckland 10, New Zealand
77–85 Fulham Palace Road, London W6 8JB, United Kingdom
2 Bloor Street East, 20th floor, Toronto, Ontario M4W 1A8, Canada
10 East 53rd Street, New York NY 10022, USA

National Library of Australia Cataloguing-in-Publication data:

Clement, Rod
    Louisa May Pickett's best show and tell ever.
    Rev. ed.
    For primary school children.
    ISBN 978 0 207 20028 1 (pbk.).
    ISBN 978 0 207 20029 8 (hbk.).
    I. Title.
    A823.3

Cover design by Matt Stanton, HarperCollins Design Studio
Internal design by Mayfly Graphics
Typeset in 18pt Bembo
Printed in China by Everbest Printing Co. Ltd on 128gsm Matt Art

6 5 4 3 2   08 09 10 11

Louisa May Pickett's
Best Show and Tell Ever

ROD
CLEMENT

For Sue

My name is Louisa May Pickett
and I have only *one* talent – Show and Tell.
At my old school I was voted
'The Most Interesting Person in Class'
three years in a row.

I have just moved to a new school.
I aim to spend all my spare time
collecting incredibly interesting
stuff and having amazing
experiences that I can share
with my new classmates.

Look out,
Bobbin Head Primary,
here I come!

Show and Tell, February 8.

My first Show and Tell at my new school.

I think I should start nice and slowly.

I don't want to look like a show-off ...

well, not on my first day.

I've decided to take my skull of the Sabre-toothed Tiger,

one of only three owned outside a museum.

Big mistake.

Jake took the head of a Tyrannosaurus Rex.

Remember, Louisa, nice guys finish last.

Show and Tell, February 15.
I can't wait to see the looks on their faces, as I'm pretty sure no one's seen a juggling mouse before.

I'm *still* not sure anyone's seen a juggling mouse –
because they were all too busy looking at Ruby's rat,

the one that tap dances *and* sings in tune!

Must try harder!

Show and Tell, February 22.

No mercy this time.

I told the class about my trip across the bay

in a wooden raft I built myself,

complete with maps

and small-scale model.

What a shame Christopher showed
a film of his trip down the Amazon,
with the help of his Indian guide!

Show and Tell, February 29.
Feeling terrific today, which is how you should be feeling
when you're dressed as a *samurai*!

Unfortunately Anthony, dressed as a warrior troll,
was feeling just a little bit better.

Show and Tell, March 7.
Brought in my parachute and described my jump
off the Sydney Harbour Bridge.

'That's right, I jumped off the Sydney Harbour Bridge,
isn't that amazing?'

No answer. I'm not sure they could hear me from up there in Julianna's
hot-air balloon. You know, the one that flew non-stop across the *Atlantic*.

Show and Tell, March 14.
My mother's meat-eating plant might have grabbed their attention
if Reginald's black rhino hadn't grabbed it first.

Hot-air balloons? Black rhinos?
This could be tougher than I thought!

Show and Tell, March 21.
Okay, no more Mr Nice Guy – it's time to take Ollie,
my pet octopus. She paints portraits with her ink.

Maybe, if she'd had time to finish the sketch, things would have been
different? *Maybe* if Lianne's giant squid had behaved itself?

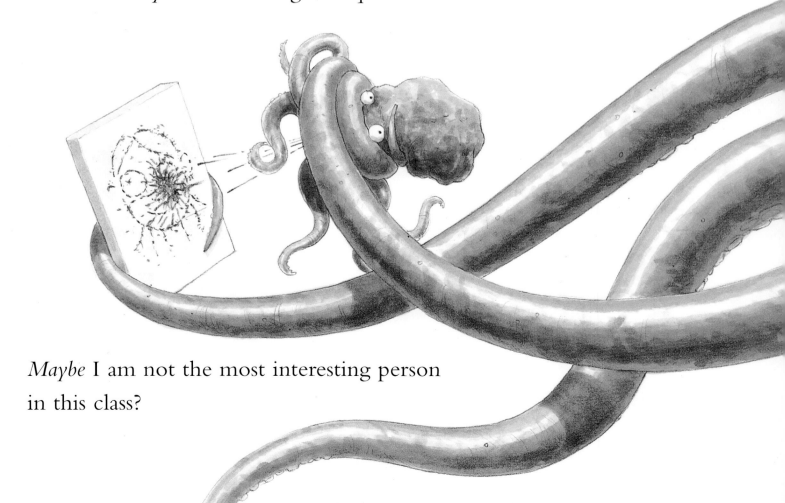

Maybe I am not the most interesting person
in this class?

Show and Tell, March 28.

This is getting serious. What's more interesting than a giant squid –
the troupe of acrobatic monkeys or the bouncing armadillo?

No   and   no.

Ah-ha! The talking chair ought to do it,
the one that recites the complete
works of William Shakespeare!

What a pity he only made it to the second page of *Hamlet* before he was drowned out by Bethany's singing fridge.

How was I to know the entire class were ABBA fans?

Show and Tell, April 4.
Soldier ants, dressed as soldiers,
sucked up by Megan's
mechanical maid.

April 11.
Eiffel Tower made
of matchsticks, burnt
down by Ishan's
Olympic torch.

April 18.
Chess-playing chimp, beaten by Chester's chess-playing chicken.

April 25.
Authentic pirate treasure chest, complete with treasure, squashed by Napat's giant golden Buddha.

Night before Show and Tell, May 1.

What should I take?

Snakes doing the alphabet?

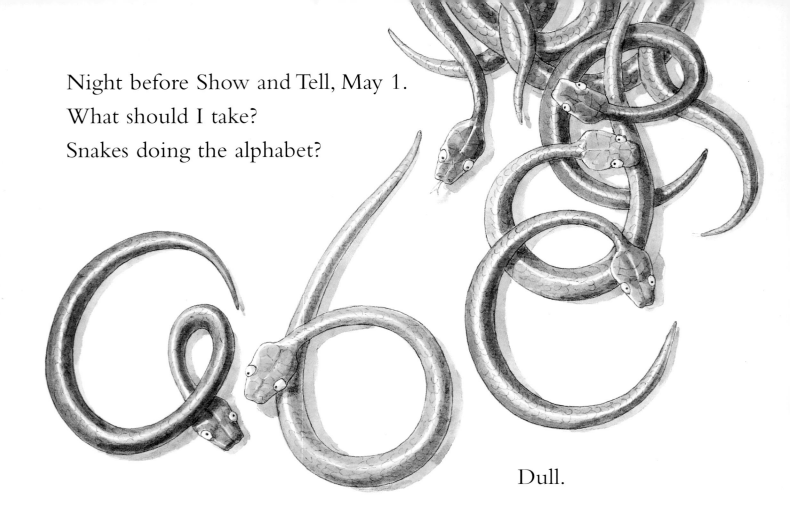

Dull.

Space suit worn by first man on the moon?

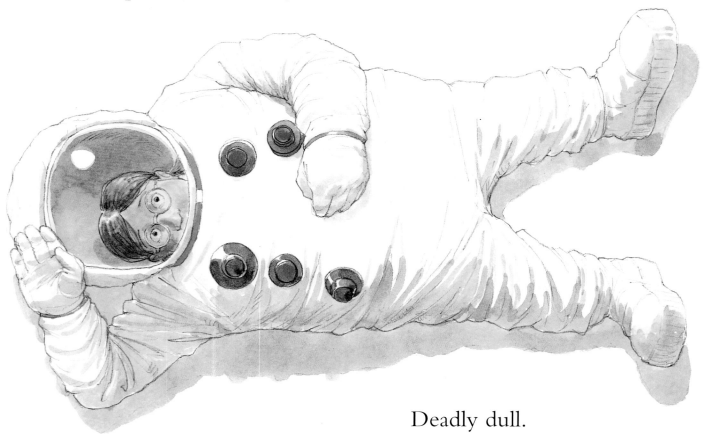

Deadly dull.

Aquatic pigeons?

Who am I kidding?

They wouldn't be able to keep their eyes open!

Starting to have
serious doubts.

Show and Tell, May 2.

Have to admit it, I don't want to go to school.

I can't compete with this lot.

All I have left is my
extremely rare pink polar
bear, the one that walks
the high wire upside
down while singing
'We all Live in a
Yellow Submarine'
backwards.

If he fails to get their attention, I'm doomed!

It's over.

No one looked.

No one listened.

Why would they?

If you think pink polar bears are rare,
wait till you see Beverly's pet gorilla!

King Kong lives!

It's official – I have just won the award for
'The Most Boring Person in Class'.

Day after Show and Tell, May 3.

That's it. I'm not going to school.

I'm running away to join the circus.

Who am I kidding – why would the circus want me?

I am *so* dull.

All I have to offer is a juggling mouse,

meat-eating plants, a parachute, a singing chair,

a painting squid, a pink polar bear

and all the other things too *boring* to mention.

I give up.

Night before Show and Tell, May 8.

Have made no effort to
do anything or find
anything all week.

Feeling a little strange since giving up —
like a huge weight has been lifted from my shoulders.

I'm not sure, but I think I like it.

Maybe I will go to school.

What have I got to lose that I haven't lost already?

Show and Tell, May 9.

'My name is Louisa May Pickett

and I have nothing to show you and nothing to tell.

I did nothing all week.

I stayed at home with my parents.

I ate.

I slept.

I sat around and

thought about ... *nothing*.

And you know what?

I loved every minute

of it!'

The class went quiet. Some of them stared.

Ms Polecki, the teacher, fell off her chair.

'Amazing!' said someone.

'Wow!' said another.

'You did nothing?'

'I did,' I replied.

'How?' they asked.

So I told them
and
for the first time *ever*,
they listened.